Sharing Danny's Dad

Written by Angela Shelf Medearis
Illustrated by Jan Spivey Gilchrist

GoodYearBooks

When my dad went to work,
I felt sad.

I went to Danny's house to play.

Danny said, "Don't feel sad.

Today we can share my dad!"

Danny's dad tickled him,

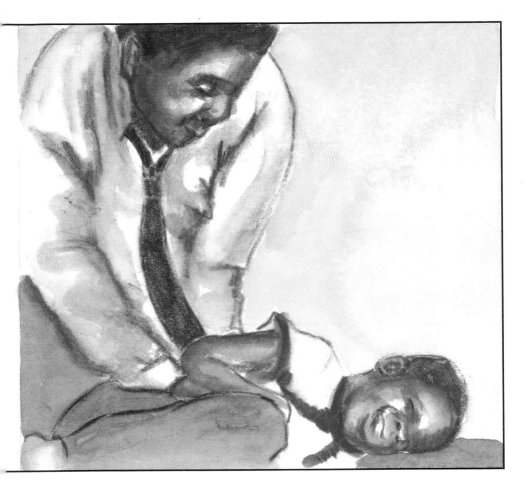

and then he tickled me.

Danny's dad threw a ball to him,

and then he threw it to me.

Danny's dad chased him,

and then he chased me.

Danny's dad pushed him
on the swing,

and then he pushed me.

We rode down the slide together,

and when we got to the bottom . . .

we shared a big hug.